Moon Jump
A COWNTDOWN
by Paula Brown

Viking

The art is collage and was prepared with ink, tempera, and colored pencil on Arches 90 lb. cold-pressed watercolor paper and color paper.

VIKING
Published by the Penguin Group
Penguin Books USA Inc., 375 Hudson Street, New York, New York 10014, U.S.A.
Penguin Books Ltd, 27 Wrights Lane, London W8 5TZ, England
Penguin Books Australia Ltd, Ringwood, Victoria, Australia
Penguin Books Canada Ltd, 10 Alcorn Avenue, Toronto, Ontario, Canada M4V 3B2
Penguin Books (N.Z.) Ltd, 182–190 Wairau Road, Auckland 10, New Zealand

Penguin Books Ltd, Registered Offices: Harmondsworth, Middlesex, England

First published in 1993 by Viking, a division of Penguin Books USA Inc.

10 9 8 7 6 5 4 3 2 1   Copyright © Paula Brown, 1993   All rights reserved

Library of Congress Cataloging-in-Publication Data   Brown, Paula. Moon jump / by Paula Brown.   p.   cm.
Summary: Ten cows compete against one another to win the first ever Moon Jump Contest.
I S B N 0 - 6 7 0 - 8 4 2 3 7 - 0   [1. Cows—Fiction. 2. Contests—Fiction.] I. Title. PZ7.B816674Mc 1993 [E]—dc20   92-22216 CIP   AC

Printed in Hong Kong   Set in 14 point Clarendon Light

To **Uri** for being there

To **Harriet** and **Henry** for their support

And special thanks to **Deborah**

Angus Le Boeuf Welcomes the Contestants

To jump over the moon,

That silvery sliver of heavenly light;

That's why all ten of you are here tonight.

So, good luck. May the best cow win.

And now, let the cowntdown begin: 10.

10 Cows Waiting to Jump Over the Moon

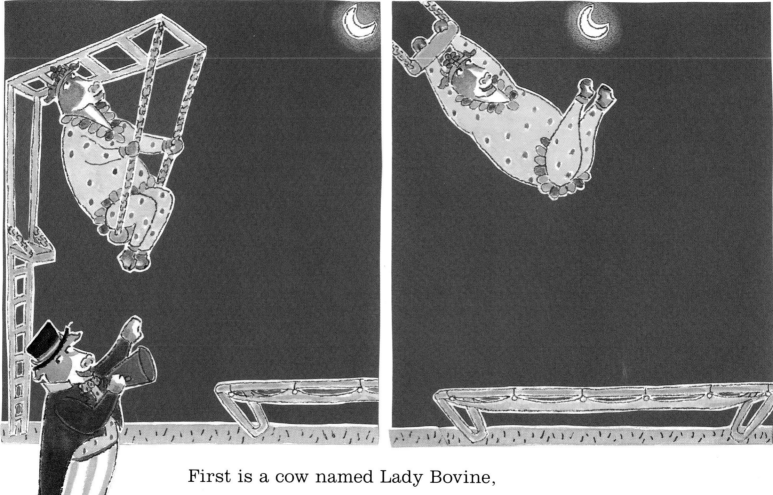

First is a cow named Lady Bovine,

On her amazing trapeze of high-rise design.

She's ready. Now watch this high flier.

There she goes . . .

Oh, no! She missed.

Too bad her trapeze wasn't higher.

Nice try, Lady Bovine.

Thank you. Now there are 9.

9 Cows Waiting to Jump Over the Moon

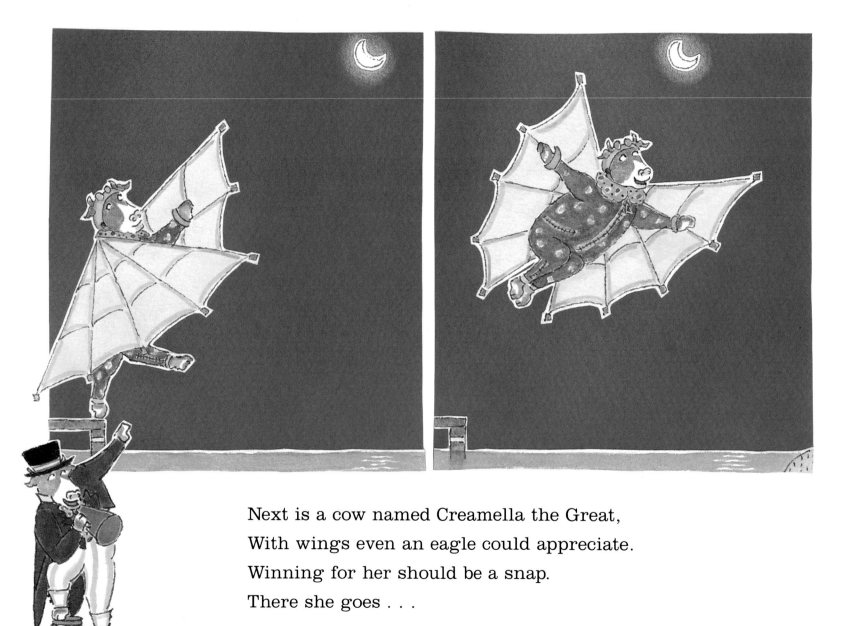

Next is a cow named Creamella the Great,

With wings even an eagle could appreciate.

Winning for her should be a snap.

There she goes . . .

Oh, no! She missed.

Too bad. Her wings were just too big to flap.

Nice try, Creamella the Great.

Thank you. Now there are 8.

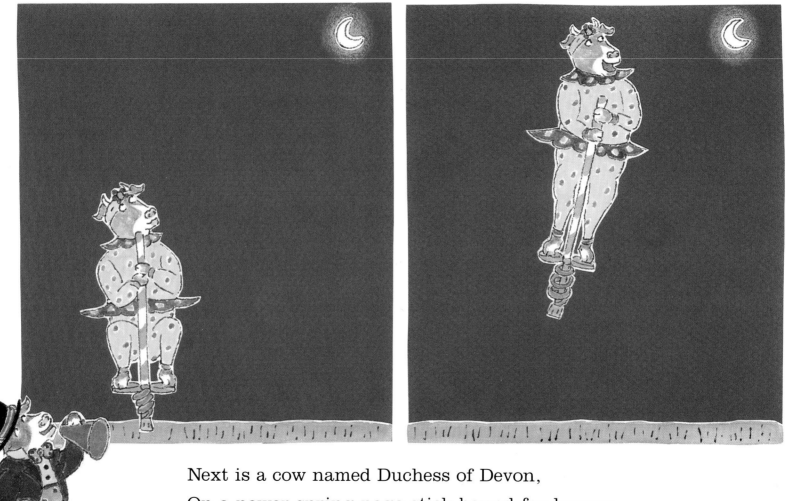

Next is a cow named Duchess of Devon,

On a power-spring pogo stick bound for heaven.

Any minute now and she'll be over the top.

There she goes . . .

Oh, no! She missed.

Too bad. The power-spring had to go and pop.

Nice try, Duchess of Devon.

Thank you. Now there are **7**.

7 Cows Waiting to Jump Over the Moon

Next is a cow named Bossie Beatrix.

To win, a mighty slingshot is what she picks.

She aims, and zing . . . flying exactly on course.

There she goes . . .

Oh, no! She missed.

Too bad. Her mighty slingshot didn't have enough force.

Nice try, Bossie Beatrix.

Thank you. Now there are **6**.

6 Cows Waiting to Jump Over the Moon

Next is a cow named Jersey Jo Jive,

On top of the world's highest high dive.

She's on her mark, she's all set to pounce.

There she goes . . .

Oh, no! She missed.

Too bad. The board needed more bounce.

Nice try, Jersey Jo Jive.

Thank you. Now there are 5.

Cows Waiting to Jump Over the Moon

Next is a cow named Queen Aberdeen of Abermor,

On a contraption like I've never seen before.

Let's watch her now as she does her stuff.

There she goes . . .

Oh, no! She missed.

Too bad. The weight didn't weigh nearly enough.

Nice try, Queen Aberdeen of Abermor.

Thank you. Now there are 4.

4 Cows Waiting to Jump Over the Moon

Next is a cow named Dairy Lee,

With a fan as tall as the tallest oak tree.

Like a heli**cow**pter, she rises from the ground.

There she goes . . .

Oh, no! She missed.

Too bad. The propeller unwound from spinning round and round.

Nice try, Dairy Lee.

Thank you. Now there are **3**.

3 Cows Waiting to Jump Over the Moon

Next is a cow named Mary La Moo,

On a **moo**torcycle, geared for a moon rendezvous.

Va-rooom . . . And she's already halfway there.

There she goes . . .

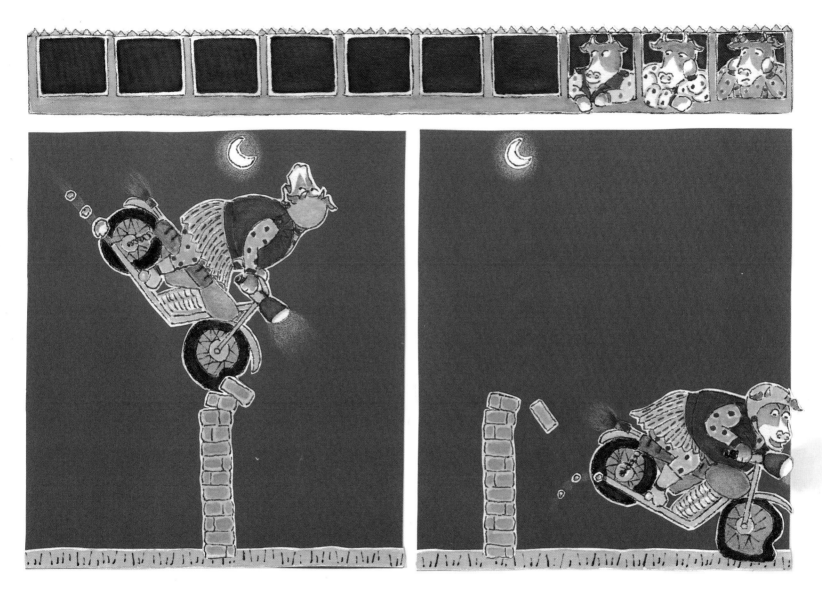

Oh, no! She missed.

Too bad. Her **moo**torcycle stalled right in midair.

Nice try, Mary La Moo.

Thank you. Now there are **2**.

Next is a cow named Guernsey Gert of Gerdun.

With her rockets, this cowsmonaut could have this contest won.

Blast-off! And moonward she streaks.

There she goes . . .

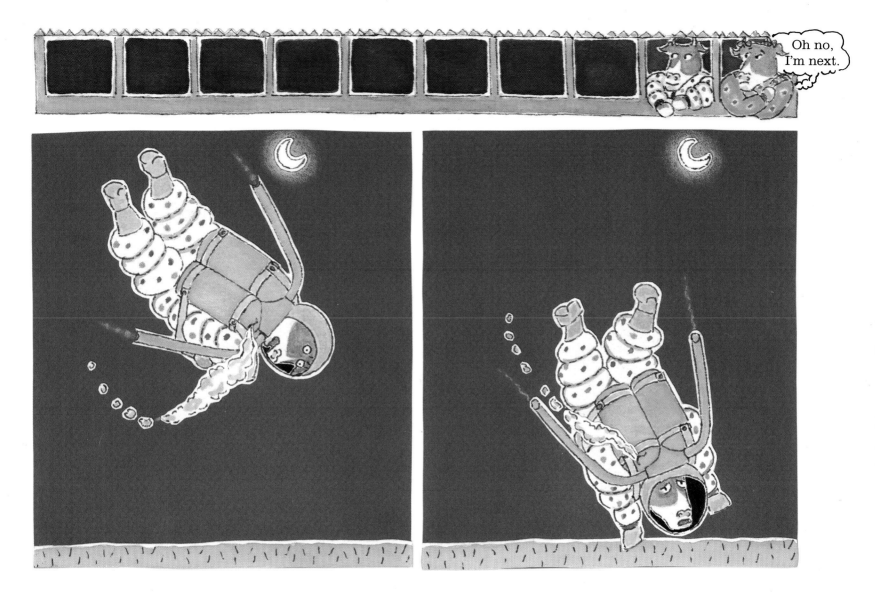

Oh, no! She missed.

Too bad. Her rockets sprang leaks.

Nice try, Guernsey Gert of Gerdun.

Thank you. Now there is 1.

Last is a cow named Little Miss Heiferton,

With her plain old, ordinary long wooden pole.

Watch now as she tries to reach her goal.

There she goes . . .

Oh, no! Her pole is bending like wire,
She's hoisting herself higher and higher,
She's up . . .
Up!

O Cows Waiting to Jump Over the Moon

Holy cow! She's up and over!

She did it! She did what's never been done.

She jumped over the moon!

Little Miss Heiferton won!

Look, here she comes now,

Three cheers for our champion cow!

Hip hip, hip hip, hip hip hooray!

The contest is over. Now there are none.

Little Miss Heiferton laughed and mooed
as she was herded onto the stage.
Then she said a few words:

"I want to thank my pole for its support
and the moon for being there.
Wow! I'm so happy."

Then, in the moonlight, everyone celebrated

all night long.

By daybreak, the moon was gone,
Angus Le Boeuf was back in the barn,
and all ten cows had hit the hay.